Boomer's Big Surprise

D0507367

For John, with love — C.W.M.

For Wes, with love — M.W.

With love to all big brothers and sisters — Boomer

No part of this publication may be reproduced in whole or in part, or stored in a retrieval system, or transmitted in any form or by any means, electronic, mechanical, photocopying, recording, or otherwise, without written permission of the publisher. For information regarding permission, write to Chronicle Books, 85 Second Street, San Francisco, CA 94105.

ISBN 0-439-13307-6

Text copyright © 1999 by Constance W. McGeorge.
Illustrations copyright © 1999 by Mary Whyte.
All rights reserved. Published by Scholastic Inc.,
555 Broadway, New York, NY 10012, by arrangement with Chronicle Books.
SCHOLASTIC and associated logos are trademarks and/or registered trademarks of Scholastic Inc.

12 11 10 9 8 7 6 5 4 3 2 1   9/9 0 1 2 3 4/0

Printed in the U.S.A.   08

First Scholastic printing, September 1999

Book design by Vandy Ritter.
Typeset in Electra and Berliner Grotesk.
The illustrations in this book were rendered in watercolor.

Boomer's Big Surprise

by Constance W. McGeorge   illustrated by Mary Whyte

SCHOLASTIC INC.
New York   Toronto   London   Auckland   Sydney
Mexico City   New Delhi   Hong Kong

Boomer had just come inside from playing in the backyard when he discovered strange things in the kitchen.

Newspapers were scattered all over the floor. A shiny new bowl was next to Boomer's dinner bowl. And beside his bed was a large box.

Just then, Boomer's family came into the kitchen. Everyone was smiling and talking all at once. A small bundle was placed gently on the floor.

Boomer wagged his tail, but no one seemed to notice. Boomer barked and barked, but no one seemed to hear. All eyes were on the bundle.

Boomer pushed forward for a peek.

The bundle wiggled. Boomer's eyes widened, and he moved closer. The bundle wiggled some more. Boomer's ears perked up, and he sniffed and sniffed.

And then, to his surprise, a little black
nose and a pink tongue appeared.
It was a *baby* Boomer!

Baby jumped up and scampered about the kitchen.
Soon, he found the shiny new bowl. It was filled with food.
Baby ate and ate.

Boomer was confused. There was no food in his bowl,
and it wasn't even time for dinner yet.

After Baby finished eating, everyone went to the living room and sat on the sofa – even Baby. Baby's back was scratched. Baby's belly was rubbed. Baby was patted again and again.

Boomer sat next to the sofa. He was not allowed to sit on it. He nudged an elbow. He pawed at a knee. Boomer wanted someone to pat him, too. But no one did.

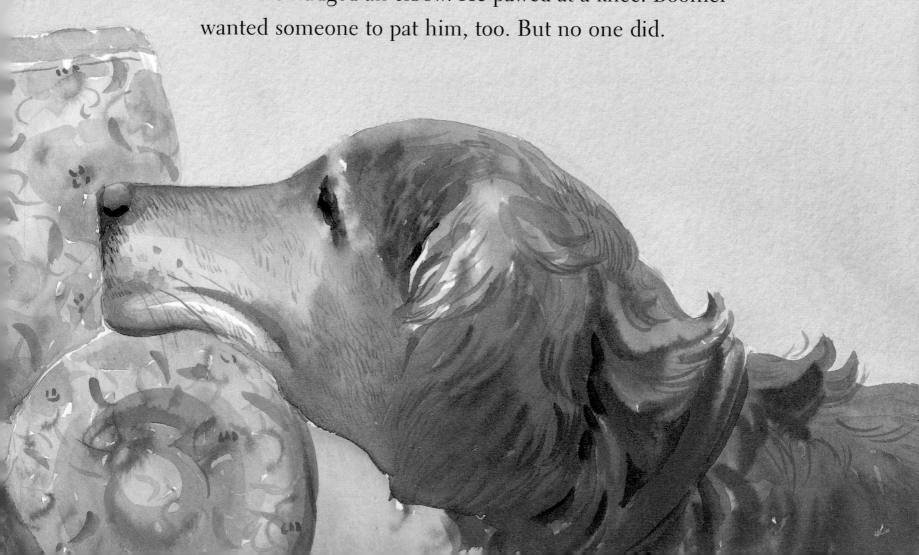

In the living room, there were new toys everywhere – bright blue balls, shiny squeaky toys, and lots of bones to chew. But the only toy Baby wanted to play with was Boomer's favorite – his old green tennis ball.

Baby made himself right at home.

Later, everyone went outside to play. Boomer was very
excited. He loved to play fetch. He waited and waited
for someone to throw him the ball. But no one did.

Finally, Boomer lay down at the far end of the yard.
He wondered if anyone would ever play with him.

But, it wasn't long before Boomer felt a lick on his nose.
He opened his eyes. There was his old green tennis ball.
And there was Baby, wagging his tail.

Boomer started across the yard, and Baby bounded after him.
At last, Boomer had someone to play with!

Boomer showed Baby how to play…

in the water …

in the dirt...

and all through the house!

When they were done playing, Boomer and Baby ate their dinners side by side. Soon it was time for bed. Everyone patted Boomer and Baby goodnight. Happy to have Baby next to him, Boomer closed his eyes and went to sleep.